TAKING A SPIN

By EMILY ARROW
Illustrations by MAARTEN LENOIR
Music by EMILY ARROW

CANTATA LEARNING

WWW.CANTATALEARNING.COM

CANTATA LEARNING

Published by Cantata Learning
1710 Roe Crest Drive
North Mankato, MN 56003
www.cantatalearning.com

Library of Congress Cataloging-in-Publication Data

Names: Arrow, Emily, author. | Lenoir, Maarten, illustrator.
Title: Taking a spin / by Emily Arrow ; illustrated by Maarten Lenoir ; music by Emily Arrow.
Description: North Mankato, MN : Cantata Learning, [2020] | Series: My feelings, my choices | Includes bibliographical references.
Identifiers: LCCN 2018053380 (print) | LCCN 2018055662 (ebook) | ISBN 9781684104215 (eBook) | ISBN 9781684104062 (hardcover) | ISBN 9781684104338 (pbk.)
Subjects: LCSH: Problem solving in children--Juvenile literature. | Problem solving--Juvenile literature.
Classification: LCC BF723.P8 (ebook) | LCC BF723.P8 A77 2020 (print) | DDC 155.5/1343--dc23
LC record available at https://lccn.loc.gov/2018053380

Book design and art direction: Tim Palin Creative
Editorial direction: Kellie M. Hultgren
Music direction: Elizabeth Draper
Music composed and produced by Emily Arrow

Printed in the United States of America.
012020 003100

ACCESS THE MUSIC!
SCAN CODE WITH MOBILE APP
CANTATALEARNING.COM

TIPS TO SUPPORT LITERACY AT HOME

WHY READING AND SINGING WITH YOUR CHILD IS SO IMPORTANT

Daily reading with your child leads to increased academic achievement. Music and songs, specifically rhyming songs, are a fun and easy way to build early literacy and language development. Music skills correlate significantly with both phonological awareness and reading development. Singing helps build vocabulary and speech development. And reading and appreciating music together is a wonderful way to strengthen your relationship.

READ AND SING EVERY DAY!

TIPS FOR USING CANTATA LEARNING BOOKS AND SONGS DURING YOUR DAILY STORY TIME

1. As you sing and read, point out the different words on the page that rhyme. Suggest other words that rhyme.
2. Memorize simple rhymes such as Itsy Bitsy Spider and sing them together. This encourages comprehension skills and early literacy skills.
3. Use the questions in the back of each book to guide your singing and storytelling.
4. Read the included sheet music with your child while you listen to the song. How do the music notes correlate to the words of the song?
5. Sing along on the go and at home. Access music by scanning the QR code on each Cantata book. You can also stream or download the music for free to your computer, smartphone, or mobile device.

Devoting time to daily reading shows that you are available for your child. Together, you are building language, literacy, and listening skills.

Have fun reading and singing!

Everybody has big feelings sometimes. If your friend takes a toy that you wanted, you might yell at them because you feel **angry**. Then you might feel sad that you hurt your friend's feelings.

But even in the middle of big feelings, we can choose what we do. The wheel of **choice** helps us remember different choices we can make when we feel upset. Watch for them as you read this book.

Are you ready to take a **spin** on the wheel of choice? Turn the page and sing along!

123
Aa
ABCD
EFGH
Walk away
Play
scissors
you're sorry
Ask them to stop
Count to ten
Talk about how you feel

Take a spin on the wheel of choice.
If you have a **problem**, give it a chance.

Take a spin on the wheel of choice.
Find a **solution**. See where it lands.

Walk away
Play rock-paper-scissors
Say you're sorry
Ask them to stop
Count to ten
Talk about how you feel

Round and round, you could walk away.
Round and round, count to ten and wait.
1 - 2 - 3 - 4 - 5 - 6 - 7 - 8 - 9 - 10: wait.

3
5 4
6
7
PARTY

Take a spin on the wheel of choice.
If you have a problem, give it a chance.

Take a spin on the wheel of choice.
Find a solution. See where it lands.

Say you're sorry

Round and round, say you're sorry first.
Round and round, play **rock-paper-scissors**.
Rock, paper, scissors, rock, paper, scissors, rock,
paper, scissors: it works!

Play rock-paper-scissors

Take a spin on the wheel of choice.
If you have a problem, give it a chance.

Take a spin on the wheel of choice.
Find a solution. See where it lands.

Round and round, ask them to stop.
Round and round, share your own thoughts.
"I think, I feel, I want, I wish."

Sometimes it helps to talk.

Say you're sorry
Ask them to stop

Sometimes it doesn't work out.
And if it doesn't work out, just spin again.
Try it now.

Walk away

Take a spin on the wheel of choice.
If you have a problem, give it a chance.

Take a spin on the wheel of choice.
Find a solution. See where it lands.

SONG LYRICS

Taking a Spin

Take a spin on the wheel of choice.
If you have a problem, give it a chance.

Take a spin on the wheel of choice.
Find a solution. See where it lands.

Round and round, you could walk away.
Round and round, count to ten and wait.
1 - 2 - 3 - 4 - 5 - 6 - 7 - 8 - 9 - 10: wait.

Take a spin on the wheel of choice.
If you have a problem, give it a chance.

Take a spin on the wheel of choice.
Find a solution. See where it lands.

Round and round, say you're sorry first.
Round and round, play rock-paper-scissors.
Rock, paper, scissors, rock, paper, scissors, rock,
paper, scissors: it works!

Take a spin on the wheel of choice.
If you have a problem, give it a chance.

Take a spin on the wheel of choice.
Find a solution. See where it lands.

Round and round, ask them to stop.
Round and round, share your own thoughts.
"I think, I feel, I want, I wish."
Sometimes it helps to talk.

Sometimes it doesn't work out.
And if it doesn't work out, just spin again.
Try it now.

Take a spin on the wheel of choice.
If you have a problem, give it a chance.

Take a spin on the wheel of choice.
Find a solution. See where it lands.

Taking a Spin

Kindie
Emily Arrow

Chorus

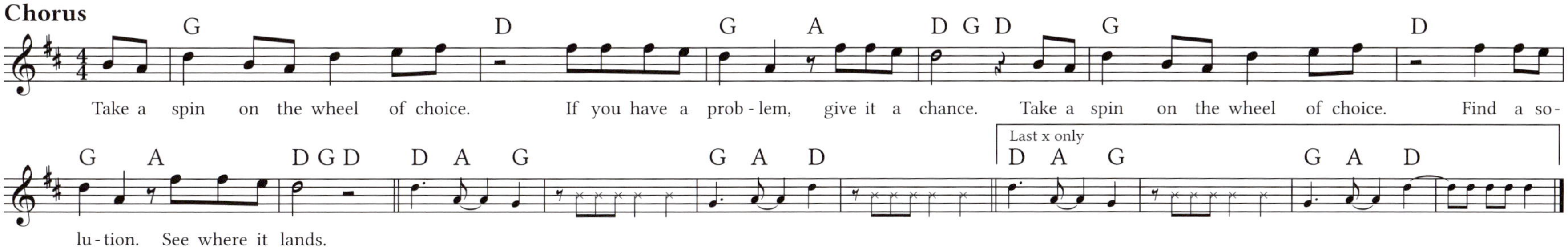

Verse

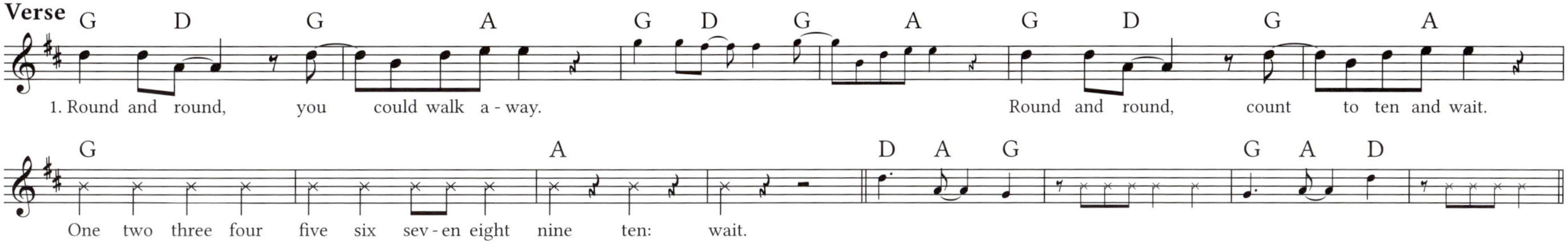

Chorus

Verse 2
Round and round, say you're sorry first.
Round and round, play rock-paper-scissors.
Rock, paper, scissors, rock, paper, scissors, rock, paper, scissors: it works!

Chorus

Verse 3
Round and round, ask them to stop.
Round and round, share your own thoughts.
"I think, I feel, I want, I wish." Sometimes it helps to talk.

Bridge

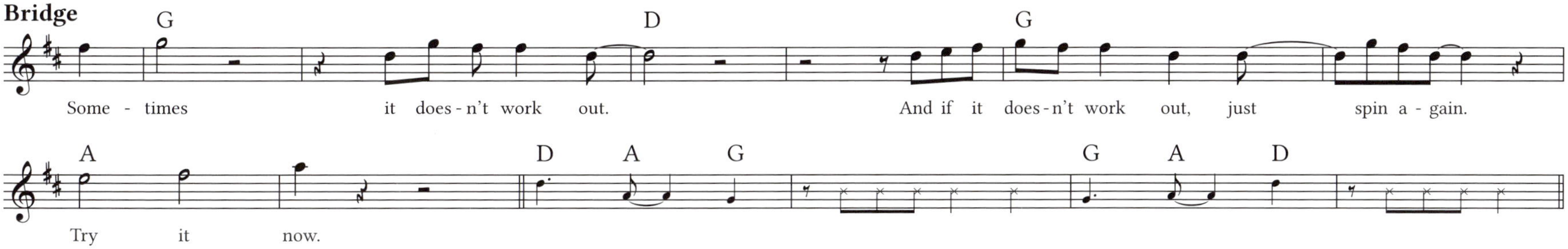

Chorus

GLOSSARY

angry—very mad

choice—something you can pick or decide to do

problem—something that needs an answer or causes unhappiness

rock-paper-scissors—a game where players make shapes with their hands

solution—a way of solving or fixing a problem

spin—a movement around in a circle

CRITICAL THINKING QUESTIONS

1. Listen to the song again. Can you think of a choice that is not described in the book? Find a friend and act it out. Does it work?
2. Make your own wheel of choice poster. Draw a circle. Then divide it like the picture on page 5. In each section, draw or write a different way that you can solve problems. Do you have a solution of your own to add to the wheel?
3. Create your own dance moves to do when you hear or sing, "Take a spin on the wheel of choice" and "Round and round." How will you move along as you listen to the song?

TO LEARN MORE

Anderson, Steven. *The More We Get Together*. North Mankato, MN: Cantata Learning, 2016.

Anstee, Ashlyn. *No, No, Gnome*. New York, NY: Simon & Schuster, 2016

Hoena, Blake. *Stretchy Shapes! Straight, Curved, and Twisty*. North Mankato, MN: Cantata Learning, 2019.

LeBox, Annette. *Peace is an Offering*. New York, NY: Penguin Young Readers Group, 2015.